NATURE UNLEASHED

HURRICANES

Louise and Richard Spilsbury

W
FRANKLIN WATTS
LONDON·SYDNEY

Franklin Watts
First published in Great Britain in 2016 by The Watts Publishing Group

Copyright © The Watts Publishing Group 2016

Credits
Series Editors: Sarah Eason and Harriet McGregor
Series Designer: Simon Borrough
Picture Researcher: Rachel Blount

Picture credits: Cover: Shutterstock: Glynnis Jones; Inside: NOAA: Debbie Larson,
NWS, International Activities 17; Shutterstock: Michael Ciranni 1, KAZMAT 23, Leonard
Zhukovsky 4–5, Zstock 6–7; Wikimedia Commons: U.S. Coast Guard photo by
Petty Officer 2nd Class NyxoLyno Cangemi 13, Sonny Day 15, NASA/Joint Typhoon
Warning Center 11, NOAA 19, 21, Presidencia de la República Mexicana 25, Eoghan
Rice/Trócaire/Caritas 27, Image courtesy of Mike Trenchard, Earth Sciences & Image
Analysis Laboratory, Johnson Space Center 7, Library of Congress/Zahner, MH 9.

Every attempt has been made to clear copyright. Should there be any inadvertent
omission please apply to the publisher for rectification.

HB ISBN: 978 1 4451 5395 7

Printed in China

FSC
MIX
Paper from
responsible sources
FSC® C104740
www.fsc.org

Franklin Watts
An imprint of
Hachette Children's Group
Part of The Watts Publishing Group
Carmelite House
50 Victoria Embankment
London EC4Y 0DZ

An Hachette UK Company
www.hachette.co.uk

www.franklinwatts.co.uk

Contents

HURRICANE DANGER

Hurricanes are the deadliest and most powerful storms on the planet. They form over warm oceans, but can blow towards land. They bring strong winds and heavy rains that cause terrible destruction.

How Dangerous?

It is hard to tell exactly how fast the winds in a hurricane blow, because these deadly storms often damage measuring equipment. Hurricane winds range from speeds of 120 kilometres per hour (kph) to more than 240 kph. The worst, most dangerous hurricane winds may reach 320 kph. Hurricane winds flatten buildings, snap power lines, pull up trees and bring rain that causes devastating **floods**. In the ocean, the winds cause huge waves that toss boats and ships around like toys. They may even throw vessels up onto the seashore.

More than 80 houses were destroyed in Breezy Point, New York, United States, by a fire that broke out when Hurricane Sandy swept through the area.

Measuring Disaster

Scientists use a number of techniques to detect hurricanes and work out where they might hit the coast, so they can warn people to **evacuate**.

Scientists must get inside hurricanes to understand how they work.

Drones are remote controlled aircraft. They fly into the **eye** of a hurricane and collect information about how hurricanes develop.

Hurricanes begin as thunderclouds.

Scientists use pictures of clouds taken by **satellites** high above the Earth's surface to work out which weather systems might become hurricanes.

Hurricanes can travel long distances.

Meteorologists use powerful computers called supercomputers to analyse billions of pieces of weather information from around the world. This helps them predict where hurricanes might happen.

Natural disasters have taken place since the Earth was formed. People have many ways of deciding what the world's worst natural disasters have been, from the deadliest disaster to the costliest. This book includes some of the worst hurricane disasters in history.

HURRICANES IN ACTION

The Saffir-Simpson Hurricane Scale ranks hurricanes from 1 to 5 based on wind speed and the damage they could cause. The least dangerous is 1 and the most dangerous is 5. This gives people a quick and clear idea of what is coming when warnings are given. Hurricanes are also named to identify them. Hurricanes are named in alphabetical order but the names never begin with the letters Q, U, X, Y or Z because few names start with these letters.

Palm trees such as these are able to bend in high winds, but hurricane force winds can completely destroy them.

Hurricane, Typhoon or Cyclone?

Hurricanes form over tropical oceans where the surface water is warm. In some places, hurricanes are known by different names. 'Hurricane' is used in the Atlantic and Northeast Pacific Oceans. In the Northwest Pacific a hurricane is called a typhoon and in the South Pacific and Indian Oceans a hurricane is called a cyclone.

How Hurricanes Form

1. Hurricanes start to form when storm clouds move over warm ocean water.

2. The warm ocean water heats the air above it. As the air warms, it starts to rise.

3. Water at the surface of the ocean **evaporates** into **water vapour**. This also rises into the air.

4. As these areas of moving air and clouds rise, they move faster and faster. They start to rotate in a spiral.

In this image of a hurricane, we can see swirling clouds and the hurricane's eye at the centre. The picture was taken from a satellite high above planet Earth.

6. When hurricanes move away from warm areas of water and towards cooler areas of land, the water vapour they carry **condenses** and turns to liquid. This water falls as rain.

5. The centre of the hurricane is calm. It is called the hurricane's eye.

The Great Galveston Hurricane of 1900 was one of the deadliest natural disasters that has ever happened in the history of the United States. Estimates of the number of people killed range from 6,000 to 12,000.

UNITED STATES

New England

Galveston

Texas

Houston

Gulf of Mexico

CUBA

Galveston, Texas

The deadly weather system that caused this hurricane was first spotted on 27 August over the Atlantic Ocean. It reached Cuba as a **tropical storm** on 3 September and moved into the south-eastern Gulf of Mexico on 5 September. As it headed west-north-west, it grew stronger and stronger. When it hit the island city of Galveston on the Texas coast late on 8 September, it was a category 4 hurricane, the second-strongest on the Saffir-Simpson Hurricane Scale.

On the Record

The hurricane caused **storm tides** 2.5–4.5 metres (m) high. Water flooded into the low-lying city of Galveston and other areas of the nearby Texas coast.

The hurricane winds blew at over 210 kph. Homes and businesses were devastated by the floods and wind. The damage to property was estimated at £22 million.

People along the Gulf Coast were warned that a hurricane was coming, but many ignored the warnings.

After making **landfall** at Galveston, the storm moved on through the Great Plains, to the Great Lakes and New England, which experienced strong wind gusts and heavy rainfall.

Before the hurricane, Galveston was an important seaport. After the hurricane, Galveston built a large wall to protect against future storms, but it was too late. By then, Houston had become the most important port.

9 TYPHOON NINA

In August 1975 an intense and devastating typhoon struck China. In the short time that Typhoon Nina made landfall, it caused dams to collapse, leading to terrible floods downstream. These killed more than 26,000 people immediately. Thousands more perished in the following days and weeks.

Henan

CHINA

Philippine Sea

Taiwan

Typhoon Nina

Disastrous Rains

The weather system that caused Typhoon Nina formed in the Philippine Sea on 29 July. It passed through Taiwan, where it killed 25 people, and hit China on 3 August. By 5 August, it reached the Henan region, where it stayed for three days. The storm dropped more rain on Henan in that time than usually falls on the region in a whole year.

On the Record

Satellite images like this one show Typhoon Nina's progress as it passed over China.

The rainwater from Typhoon Nina fell at a record rate of 19 centimetres (cm) per hour.

The huge Banqiao Dam on the River Ru was 118 m tall and held back about 492 million **cubic metres** (cu m) of water. It collapsed because it could not release water as fast as its **reservoir** behind it was filling.

The typhoon's heavy rains made more than 60 dams and reservoirs collapse, causing many more terrible floods.

When the Banqiao Dam collapsed, a wall of water 10 m high and 11 km wide rushed down the river channel at 50 kph. The 10,000 inhabitants of the town of Daowencheng were killed instantly.

As well as those killed in the floods, 145,000 people died from diseases caught by using **contaminated** river water or from starvation after crops were ruined.

11

8 HURRICANE KATRINA

Hurricane Katrina formed during the United States's 2005 Atlantic hurricane season. It was a category 5 hurricane and killed 1,850 people. At the time, it was the deadliest hurricane to have hit the United States for 75 years.

UNITED STATES

Biloxi

New Orleans

Florida

Gulf of
Mexico

Hurricane Katrina

Caribbean Sea

Gaining Strength

Hurricane Katrina formed over the Caribbean Sea on 23 August and made landfall in Florida on 25 August where it killed nine people. Next, it moved on to the Gulf of Mexico, where the warm waters helped it to double in size. By the time it reached New Orleans early in the morning of 29 August its wind speeds were 200 kph and it was dropping torrential rain. The hurricane caused 151 billion dollars (about 84 billion pounds) of damage. Today, many areas have been rebuilt but some people have never returned and houses still lie abandoned in some parts of the city.

On the Record

The winds from Hurricane Katrina snapped trees, blew out windows and threw furniture from homes on to the streets. Broken power lines caused fires.

New Orleans lies below **sea level** and had banks of earth called levees built around it to prevent flooding. However, the heavy rains caused such severe flooding that the levees broke and water flooded 80 per cent of the city.

In some places in New Orleans, flood waters were 6 m deep.

Seawater filled homes. It also spread poisonous snakes, mud, rocks and **debris** from damaged buildings all over the city.

As Hurricane Katrina moved along the coast, it caused more damage in Louisiana, Mississippi and Alabama. It tossed boats ashore and filled towns with mud and sand. In the coastal town of Biloxi, a **storm surge** 9 m high killed 30 people.

7 TYPHOON BOPHA

Families lost their homes, possessions and many lost their lives when Typhoon Bopha struck the island of Mindanao in the Philippines on 3 December 2012. This typhoon was also the most expensive to hit the Philippines and cost the country £740 million.

Typhoon Bopha

PHILIPPINES

Mindanao

A Vulnerable Country

The Philippines gets lots of typhoons because it is located in the middle of a huge area of warm water in the Pacific Ocean. The country consists of more than 7,000 islands, which are vulnerable to flooding when typhoons cause storm surges. Unusually, the large southern island of Mindanao is rarely in the direct path of typhoons. In 2012 its luck ran out. In the months following the typhoon, the European Union and governments from Australia, China and other countries sent aid to the island.

On the Record

Typhoon Bopha rated category 5 on the Saffir-Simpson Hurricane Scale. It was so powerful it was called a 'super typhoon'. Millions of people were in the storm's path.

The high winds, flooding and **landslides** caused by heavy rains from Typhoon Bopha killed around 1,900 people and affected over 6.2 million more.

Trees were uprooted and fragile houses were blown away on Mindanao.

Over 24 cm of rain fell near the coast of eastern Mindanao, where the typhoon first hit the island.

The typhoon brought wind gusts of 210 kph. People said wind blew corrugated iron roofs from buildings and threw them through the air like 'flying machetes'.

In the hardest-hit areas, almost 95 per cent of the roads, homes and crops were destroyed.

6 HURRICANE MITCH

Hurricane Mitch devastated parts of Central America in late October 1998. It rated 5 on the Saffir-Simpson Hurricane Scale for more than 33 hours, making it one of the most dangerous and destructive hurricanes ever recorded.

Hurricane Mitch

MEXICO

GUATEMALA
EL SALVADOR
COSTA RICA

HONDURAS
NICARAGUA

Deadly Rains

The storm killed more than 11,000 people, mainly in Honduras and Nicaragua, but also in Guatemala, El Salvador, Mexico and Costa Rica. Thousands more were left missing, presumed dead. Most of the people who died were killed in the terrible floods caused by the enormous amount of rain that the storm released. The heavy rains caused more than 50 rivers to flood. Aid agencies provided funds to rebuild schools, hospitals, roads and homes. However, once the hurricane stopped being featured in the news, the redevelopment slowed down.

On the Record

Hurricane Mitch moved slowly over land from 29 October to 3 November and released up to 10 cm of rain per hour. In some places, almost 2 m of rain fell during that time.

The heavy rains washed earth into rivers, blocking them and causing floods that washed away people, buildings, roads and bridges.

This flood damage along the River Choluteca was caused by Hurricane Mitch.

The floods and landslides damaged many thousands of homes and buildings, leaving millions of people without somewhere to live.

The heavy rains caused a lake filling the crater at the top of Casita volcano, in Nicaragua, to overflow, which made the sides of the volcano collapse. The landslide completely buried at least four villages around the volcano and killed up to 2,000 people.

5 TYPHOON TIP

On 12 October 1979 Typhoon Tip grew to become a record-breaking typhoon. It was a category 5 super typhoon and was enormous. It had a diameter of 2,173 km, which is almost half the area of the mainland United States. At its peak, while the typhoon swirled over the open waters of the western Pacific, the eye of Typhoon Tip was more than 15 km wide.

JAPAN

Tokyo

Typhoon Tip

Fast and Furious

Tip was the strongest typhoon to hit Japan's main island in over 10 years. At their fastest, winds from Tip blew at 306 kph. Luckily, the typhoon's strength and speed dropped before it hit the heavily populated regions of southern Japan, avoiding a high death toll. Typhoon Tip killed 86 people but injured hundreds more.

Tip caused widespread flooding that destroyed more than 20,000 homes in Japan. Over 11,000 people were left homeless. The heavy rains also caused 600 landslides in the mountains.

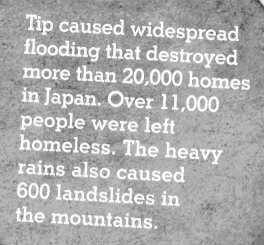

A total of 40 US hurricane hunter aircraft missions, similar to these, were flown into Typhoon Tip, making it one of the most closely studied typhoons in history.

Typhoon Tip made tall buildings in the capital city, Tokyo, sway from side to side.

Typhoon Tip's winds toppled a petrol storage tank, causing an explosion and fire that spread quickly through a US Marine Corps camp at Mount Fuji. The fire killed 13 people and injured dozens more.

19

4 HURRICANE CAMILLE

The swirling winds of Hurricane Camille formed from a tropical storm that started in the Caribbean, west of the Cayman Islands, on 14 August 1969. By the time it hit Bay Saint Louis in Mississippi, United States, shortly before midnight on 17 August it was a category 5 hurricane.

Virginia

UNITED STATES

Bay Saint Louis

Gulf of Mexico

CAYMAN ISLANDS

Hurricane Camille

Storm Warnings

Although meteorologists were not sure what path the hurricane would take, they warned more than 150,000 people to evacuate their homes. Most people followed the advice and left the danger zones in time. Some people stayed behind; more than 250 of them were killed.

On the Record

Camille's gales were so strong they knocked out all wind-recording equipment. Experts estimate that its wind speeds peaked at more than 320 kph. The high winds reduced many buildings to rubble.

Hurricane Camille created waves in the Gulf of Mexico that were more than 21 m high.

Hurricane Camille was one of the strongest hurricanes to hit the United States and it wrecked even huge ships like these in Gulfport, Mississippi.

Before the hurricane moved out into the Atlantic Ocean on 20 August, Camille dropped 30–50 cm of rain in parts of Virginia. It created floods and mudslides along the foothills of the Blue Ridge Mountains.

After Hurricane Camille, people from the Gulf Coast complained that warnings did not give clear information about how strong hurricanes were expected to be. This led to the creation of the Saffir-Simpson Hurricane Scale.

3 LABOR DAY HURRICANE

The force of the Labor Day Hurricane that hit the United States on 2 September 1935 was so great that people caught in the open were blasted with sand that stripped the clothing from them. The hurricane's destruction was focused on the Florida Keys area, where it caused a path of devastation 64 km wide.

UNITED STATES

Florida
Florida Keys ● BAHAMAS

Labor Day Hurricane

Too Late to Escape

The hurricane began as a weak tropical storm east of the Bahamas. It grew bigger and stronger as it headed west over the warm waters of the Gulf Stream. Forecasters thought it was heading south. By the time they realised otherwise, it was too late to evacuate people. When the hurricane made landfall at the Florida Keys, a chain of small islands off the southern coast of Florida, it had become a deadly and destructive category 5 hurricane.

On the Record

Experts estimate that winds of up to 320 kph blew near and over the Florida Keys, with some gusts even faster than that.

The hurricane caused a strong storm tide consisting of a wall of water about 5.5 m high.

The storm tide washed up on to the Keys and destroyed buildings, roads, viaducts and bridges.

The hurricane killed at least 485 people. About half were residents and visitors; half were First World War **veterans** who were living in tent camps, helping to build bridges between the islands.

The high winds and storm tide also destroyed railway lines and even swept a train off its tracks. The eleven-car train had been sent to evacuate about 260 of the First World War veterans working in the area. All but the locomotive engine were washed off the tracks.

23

2 HURRICANE PATRICIA

In 2015 the category 5 Hurricane Patricia became the strongest hurricane to reach Mexico in more than fifty years. It blasted the coast with winds of over 320 kph and was one of the most powerful hurricanes ever recorded.

MEXICO

Hurricane Patricia

Powerful Patricia

In 2015 the eastern Pacific was warmer than usual, which may have contributed to the power of Hurricane Patricia. Fortunately, the hurricane did not hit large population centres and people were warned in time to evacuate. This meant that, although Hurricane Patricia was ferocious, it killed only six people. Tourist resorts reopened gradually but away from these areas there was much work to do to rebuild homes, roads and farms.

On the Record

Mexican authorities warned all towns and villages in Patricia's path to evacuate. Thousands of tourists and local people left the danger zone and moved into shelters.

Airports were closed and homes and shop fronts were barricaded for protection.

Overall, more than 10,000 homes such as these in Colima, Mexico were damaged or destroyed by Hurricane Patricia.

Around 405 **square kilometres** (sq km) of farmland was affected and plantain, banana and papaya crops were ruined.

Strong winds tore roofs off houses, pulled up, snapped and stripped nearly all trees, and left hillsides bare. Power poles and pylons were crumpled by the winds.

Heavy rains caused widespread flooding. Many more houses were flooded as rivers burst their banks.

1 TYPHOON HAIYAN

An average of 20 typhoons hit the Philippines each year but Haiyan was more memorable than most. Typhoon Haiyan was one of the most powerful – if not the most powerful – tropical cyclones ever to strike land.

CHINA

Typhoon Haiyan

VIETNAM

Tacloban

Palau

PHILIPPINES

A Force of Nature

When Haiyan made landfall in the Philippines on 8 November 2013, it was a category 5 hurricane. Its wind blasted the area at speeds of around 315 kph. The winds, floods and storm surge caused by Haiyan killed 7,300 people and destroyed many of the country's coastal farming and fishing communities. Many people in the Philippines have rebuilt their homes and lives since the Haiyan cyclone. However, the entire area is still vulnerable to typhoons.

On the Record

Typhoon Haiyan caused a storm surge that was so huge and powerful that it washed ships on to the shore and rolled a 30-m rock up a beach.

The storm surge forced a wall of water 7.5 m high into the city of Tacloban, on the north-east tip of the island of Leyte. The island is only 5 m above sea level. The water swept away people and buildings, leaving a sea of mud and debris in its wake.

Haiyan – and two tropical storms that passed through the area around the same time – dumped huge amounts of rain on the central Philippines. Some parts of Leyte got as much as 70 cm of rain.

The central Philippines were worst hit, but more than 16 million people in total were affected by the event in Palau, the Philippines, Vietnam and China.

More people died in the city of Tacloban than in any other part of the Philippines.

27

WHERE IN THE WORLD?

This map shows the location of the hurricanes, typhoons and cyclones featured in this book.

ATLANTIC
OCEAN

Hurricane Camille

Hurricane Katrina

Great Galveston Hurricane

Labor Day Hurricane

Hurricane Patricia

Hurricane Mitch

PACIFIC OCEAN

Read the case studies about Haiyan (2013), the number one typhoon in this book, and the Great Galveston Hurricane (1900), which is number 10. How do they differ?

What facts can you find in this book to support the argument that human actions can affect the amount of damage inflicted by hurricanes?

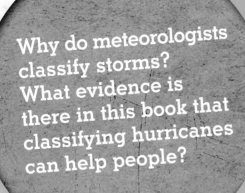

Why do meteorologists classify storms? What evidence is there in this book that classifying hurricanes can help people?

Typhoon Tip

Typhoon Nina

Typhoon Bopha

Typhoon Haiyan

INDIAN OCEAN

Where and how do hurricanes form? What makes them stronger and bigger?

How would you explain the difference between a hurricane, a cyclone and a typhoon?

GLOSSARY

condenses turns from a gas to a liquid

contaminated made dirty or poisonous

cubic metres (cu m) volume; 1 cu m is a cube that is 1 metre on each side

dams barriers built to hold back river waters and raise their levels

debris loose, waste material

drones remotely controlled aircraft that can do tasks such as take photographs from the air

evacuate to get away from an area that is dangerous to somewhere that is safe

evaporates turns from a liquid into a gas

eye the calm centre of a hurricane

floods when areas of land that are usually dry are suddenly covered in water

hurricane season the time of year when hurricanes usually happen

landfall reaching land

landslides collapses of masses of earth or rock from mountains or cliffs

meteorologists scientists who study the weather

reservoir an artificial lake where water is collected and stored, often behind a dam

Saffir-Simpson Hurricane Scale the scale by which the strength of a hurricane, typhoon or cyclone is measured

satellites objects in space that travel around the Earth

sea level the average height of the ocean's surface

square kilometres (sq km) area; 1 sq km is a square that has sides 1 km long

storm surge an abnormal rise of water generated by a hurricane or other storm

storm tides the water level rise due to the combination of storm surges and the tides

tropical storm a powerful storm that begins in the tropics; its winds are not as strong as those of a hurricane

veterans people who fought in a war

water vapour water in the form of gas

FURTHER READING

Books

Extreme Weather (National Geographic Kids),
Thomas M. Kostigen, National Geographic Society

Hurricane & Tornado (Eyewitness), DK Children

The Superstorm Hurricane Sandy (True Books),
Josh Gregory, Scholastic

Websites

Watch video clips about hurricane formation and the terrible
after-effects at:
www.bbc.co.uk/science/earth/natural_disasters/hurricane

Visit the National Geographic Kids website for 10 fascinating
hurricane facts:
www.ngkids.co.uk/science-and-nature/Hurricanes

Unlock the history of naming hurricanes at:
**www.weatheronline.co.uk/reports/wxfacts/History-of-
Hurricane-Names.htm**

Note to parents and teachers
Every effort has been made by the Publisher to ensure that
these websites contain no inappropriate or offensive material.
However, because of the nature of the Internet, it is impossible
to guarantee that the contents of these sites will not be altered.
We strongly advise that Internet access is supervised by a
responsible adult.

INDEX

These are the lists of contents for each title in *Nature Unleashed*:

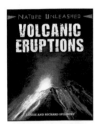

Volcanic Eruptions

Volcano Danger • Volcanoes in Action • Mount St. Helens • Pinatubo • El Chichón • Mount Vesuvius • Santa Maria • Nevado del Ruiz • Mount Pelee • Krakatau • Santorini • Mount Tambora • Where in the World? • Glossary • For More Information • Index

Earthquakes

Earthquake Danger • Earthquakes in Action • San Francisco, 1906 • Nepal, 2015 • Manjil-Rudbar, Iran, 1990 • Peru, 1970 • Kashmir, 2005 • Sichuan, 2008 • Japan, 1923 • Messina, Italy, 1908 • Tangshan, 1976 • Haiti ,2010 • Where in the World? • Glossary • For More Information • Index

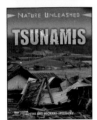

Tsunamis

Tsunami Danger • Tsunamis in Action • Flores Sea, Indonesia, 1992 • Chile, 1960 • Nankaido, Japan, 1946 • Tokaido, Japan 1923 • Papua New Guinea • San-Riku, Japan, 1933 • Andaman Sea-East Coast, 1941 • Moro Gulf, Philippines, 1976 • Japan, 2011 • Indian Ocean, 2004 • Where in the World? • Glossary • For More Information • Index

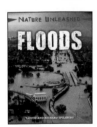

Floods

Flood Danger • Floods in Action • Mississippi Floods • Pakistan Floods, 2010 • Johnstown, 1889 • North Sea Floods, 1953 • North India Floods, 2013 • Vargas Tragedy, Venezuela, 1999 • Bangladesh, 1974 • Yangtse River Flood, 1998 • Ganges Delta, 1970 • Yellow River, China, 1931 • Where in the World? • Glossary • For More Information • Index

Hurricanes

Wind and Storm Danger • Tropical Storms in Action • Great Galveston Hurricane, 1900 • Typhoon Nina, 1975 • Hurricane Katrina, 2005 • Typhoon Bopha, 2012 • Hurricane Mitch, 1998 • Typhoon Tip, 1979 • Hurricane Camille, 1969 • Labor Day Hurricane, 1935 • Hurricane Patricia, 2015 • Typhoon Haiyan, 2013 • Where in the World? • Glossary • For More Information • Index

Wildfires

Fire Danger • Fires in Action • 2010 Russia • Ash Wednesday, 1983 • Landes Forest, 1949 • Black Saturday, 2009 • Miramichi, 1825 • Black Dragon, 1987 • Matheson Fire, 1916 • Cloquet Fire, 1918 • Peshtigo Fire, 1871 • Indonesia, 2015 • Where in the World? • Glossary • For More Information • Index